THE WEIG

The Weight Of My Raggedy Skin

DALE ZIEROTH

POLESTAR
BOOK PUBLISHERS

THE WEIGHT OF MY RAGGEDY SKIN

Published by
Polestar Book Publishers, PO Box 69382, Station K,
Vancouver, B.C.,
V5K 4W6   604-251-9718

Distributed by
Raincoast Book Distribution Ltd., 112 East 3rd Avenue,
Vancouver, B.C.,
V5T 1C8   604-873-6581

Canadian Cataloguing in Publication Data
Zieroth, Dale.
The weight of my raggedy skin
Poems.
ISBN 0-919591-67-1
I. Title.
PS8599.I47W4 1991   C811'.54   C91-091587-3
PR9199.3.Z53W4 1991

Acknowledgements
Published with the assistance of the Canada Council and the
British Columbia Cultural Services Branch

Some of these poems (sometimes in earlier versions) have
appeared in *Canadian Literature, Malahat Review, Margin,
Orbis, Quarry, Taproot, West Coast Review, The Dry Wells of
India* (Harbour, 1989), *Garden Varieties* (Cormorant, 1988),
More Garden Varieties (Aya Press, 1989), and *Paperwork*
(Harbour, 1991).

Special thanks to Janet Allwork, Bonnie Bauder, Gillian
Harding-Russell, Maurice Hodgson, Richard Lemm, Anne
Marriott, Susan McCaslin, Jim Polk, Holley Rubinsky, Susan
Wasserman, Tom Wayman, Diana Wegner, Douglas College,
and the Banff Centre.

Cover design and illustration by Jim Brennan
Interior design by Julian Ross
Typeset by Woodward Associates
Author photograph by Margery Zieroth
Printed and bound in Canada by Gagne

This book is for
my family
and the Waldorf poetry group

Books by Dale Zieroth
Clearing: Poems from a Journey (1973)
Mid-River (1981)
When the Stones Fly Up (1985)

CONTENTS

GOOD CITIZEN

The Big One   / 11
Home   / 12
On Or About Midnight   / 13
A Short History of Housekeeping   / 14
Phone Call   / 15
Death of the Violin   / 16
Roses   / 17
California   / 18
My Bones Read: National Geographic   / 19
Train   / 21
Strike Pay   / 22
Our Negotiator Speaks to Theirs   / 23
Rhetoric   / 24
Three Wishes   / 25
Poem Facing Evening   / 26

APHASIA

Afternoon and Evening   / 37
Aphasia   / 38
Flying Back From Solemn Duties   / 39
Top Drawer   / 40
Sins of Omission   / 42
David Dale   / 43
Sibling Rivalry   / 44
Debbie's Piano   / 45
Violence   / 46
The Mother Prone ✦   / 47
Advising ✦✦   / 48
Reading Late ✦✦✦   / 49
Remembering Frank ✦✦✦✦   / 50
Postscript: Sarah ✦✦✦✦✦   / 51

THE WEIGHT OF MY RAGGEDY SKIN

Heart Takes / 55
Journey / 64
Horoscope / 65
Here on the Coast / 66
Stories of Loathing / 67
The Man With the Lawn Mower / 68
The Shadow / 70
Stories From the Life of Flesh / 72
Destroyer of Atmospheres / 75
Winter Residence / 76
The Dead Are With Us / 77
Accident / 78

GOOD CITIZEN

THE BIG ONE

News item: Experts say there is a possibility that B.C. will be hit by the largest recorded quake in history.
—*Vancouver Sun, April 14, 1990*

A 747 has just taken off
for Tokyo (another zone of fire),
and beneath the safety of the wings
' my city falls
where the Big One
has come walking.
A sudden pitching down of glass
re-arranges
               the continent
down to the vowel
in the last living thought
now just wind perhaps
visiting
where walls might have been.

Ground failure
comes down upon my head.
This is an ancient village still.
If I am to live here
some part of me must fly.
Those living will take with them
perhaps one of my children
as they flee weeping
out of this desert.

Meanwhile I travel in faith
on the bridges of my city:
Lions Gate, Second Narrows,
Granville, Burrard, Puttallo,
Port Mann, Alex Fraser, Queensborough
and those smaller, nameless ones
under which I have seen children explode
into laughter as boys dump
an old chair into the stream,
on its way to the ocean
the last of its reclining done.

HOME

At the break-up of ice
a dog is barking; a star
comes climbing out
from its cold space.
Mosquito Creek smells
more firmly of mud
overflowing and set to begin its brew.
I almost stop for this.

Minutes from now
I'll step through
and fresh-faced
greet steam in the kitchen
rushing to taste
on my skin its wild
                              outside cousin
who comes up now from ice
through the alder-ready air.

Chili on the stove,
salad and Avalon
milk in the fridge, expectant
faces in the light where
I cross a room, drop
my bag, pull down the blinds,
toss and turn
what's left
                    here on the 15th street
to reach night.

ON OR ABOUT MIDNIGHT

. . . the tall lamplight
creeps palely down to blanch the grass
and send thin roots
into Mosquito Creek Lane
where my daughter walks.

Off the bus and through
the Buy-Low parking lot for pale light
from scattered, buzzing poles
beneath which she hurries,
girl in the dark.

Later if we share pink lemonade
in a few words we see
I have not kept pace
with her own will
to keep harm away.

Her speed I remember then,
the quick dancer's legs
and how they can leap, bend
and challenge.

But when she next is gone
I remember, too, the malignant grass
along which she must run.

A SHORT HISTORY OF HOUSEKEEPING

A short history of housekeeping
includes anguish, stink, Windex,
scrub, and difficulties
in the division of labour.
Is it really my turn?
Are these my hands
about to perform?

Likely your history
would involve a mother,
living or dead, but furious
when the taps won't gleam.
When you took up the broom
on your own, what message
did you forever after
play back?

List your achievements here:
the swishing down the drain of hair;
thumping stairs
with vacuum, pulling its
reluctant nose; collecting
from all floors; and listening
as machines start singing
in that wrong, broken note.
Is this where fathers come in?

PHONE CALL

My wife and two daughters
are in the bathroom: one in the tub,
one talking, one on the can.
What can I do, but knock gently
announce through the door
the phone's for one of them, the receiver
held against my hip.
The usual amazement I'm feeling
—and how it might have been,
chances taken
or turned away from.

Whose myth is this anyway?
What light falls on the man by the door?
What beam would gently paint him in,
around his feet untidy toys,
towels? Would he be better done
some darker hue, the stairwell
open like a maw for him?

"She'll call you back . . ."
And back and back, to where his own
good self stood years before, strange
child untouchable now in that first time
strange time.
His flesh cannot recall
but moves on and on in light, in love
bearing departure in mind.

DEATH OF THE VIOLIN

. . . in our house came after four years.
She had practiced—and not practiced—
long enough to (finally) make music.
She had entertained my father and mother,
and I had been proud of the songs
she had coaxed from those harsh strings.
She was, however, not staying with it.
We could no longer continue with
reminders, because reminders would be
nagging, and we wanted discipline
on her part: we wanted her to bring her will
into play.

November is a hard month to give up anything,
especially if you have held it
four years, watched it grow in your arms
until you knew just how
to make the music leap.
My own father's violin hangs on the wall
and I remember when he played,
touching strings, jabbing
at the notes until the instrument
became a fiddle, and around him
guitars and accordions
filled up the family with their talk.

Once when she played,
his violin played back,
reverberating on the wall: just once
that calling note. Then silence
filled up now with rain.
Arguments about who's supporting whom
fade, but stay, fill the air,
can't move gently into change.
And someone's disclaiming all reason
and another's volume rises to the shriek.

ROSES

Flowers at the door
red roses
a dozen, long-stemmed,
in a box. They reach out, are held out
to my daughter's beaming.
Each trimmed, fresh and dark,
wrapped up, snuggled
next to fern and greens, overflowing its part
in this gentle romance,
this American movie with Steve
the hero curly in the right damp way
stepping into a florist's
counting one, two, three.
                                        Spring
and that
spurt of blood energy even I can see
later, outside,
the forsythia waving stiffly by the fence:
Mr. Finch in full throat, his mate
plucking up busted-cassette tape
and streaming toward her nest, the boys
under twelve catching sight of this
entangled flying
and whooping as they raise their sticks
and run.

CALIFORNIA

For three days his daughter
has been away from the house
—in California, phoning home
to tell about the palm trees.
He could almost imagine
touching the bark of that curved exotica.
Since she left: the cat broke its other leg
and would need the SPCA
to make it work; the muffler fell
and his mechanic put on a hat
and went under the car in the rain
to tell of the cost of rust.

The real news: he feels
a silence come toward him
now that he has reached
and found the ground
nearer than remembered.
Only a teen-ager
can swallow the world
and dance all night.

He gathers up the clutter
that settles into a house.
He quarrels with it,
the dropped clothes, the ditched boots,
the wet towels pitched
onto the floor. He hovers, too,
above her travelling form as she passes through
country he has never seen, as she
absorbs what makes her strange.

MY BONES READ: NATIONAL GEOGRAPHIC

The chiropractor
keeps an extra set of bones
under his couch, in the office
with the dull abstracts
on the off-white walls.
When I walk in
those bones rattle
in recognition.

If I have been gone
too long, he snaps me sideways,
pops my spine,
measures and mumbles
behind my inadequate back.
Doctor, I am trying to relax
here on your couch,
but fear I'll break
all over your shoes.
One sudden twist
and the bones of the neck fly.
I have only recently
taken this man
into my aching life.

Waiting, we slip
through magazines, examine each other
and estimate the over-bookings.
My spine remembers where it is.
My flesh wishes to crawl
but the bones
stand up and walk forward
grinning. I read on:

when the flesh falls
and I'm revealed for what I am,
curled into the fetus
of calcium, sifted over,
photographed, numbered
and taken up from the sand
to be lowered into the glass case

—I'll not be present
before the prying eyes
of the next world coming
(Come right this way).

TRAIN

We are good citizens
to handle ourselves without touching.
The iron dogs
howl at every bend;
the suburbs
rise and lower along the track.
The girl's
dark shining hair
the shock inside
the impulse to reach the hand out—

Love of self
is a dark one, two-headed.
Which way takes us next?
Cross into another life
with the single fumbled touch?
I won't seek you out,
men and women of the city
so eager to leave one another,
but in our haste upon transit
we collide and move away,
and the self
sparks and is sharpened.

STRIKE PAY

How grateful can you be
for one piece of paper?
I remember the fine old adage
about three months' salary
to float you through.

As an individual
I take my pay
on nasty cold morning shifts,
decide what sign
to dangle in front,
which way to block entrances
or what exactly to say
to those with higher principles
who cross.
I rail and complain
—and balance my cheque book
quickly this month.

A group in anger
can sing a tribal tune,
and I've been told administration
is cracking soon.
Brick by brick, I expect;
vaporized some morning
so when the fogs lift off the Fraser
perhaps I'll not even see
the place where once my work
went straight into the bank—
electronic money
I neither touch nor until now
touches me.

OUR NEGOTIATOR SPEAKS TO THEIRS

Let's be clear about this:
this isn't me sitting here
but all of us embodied in me.
I am the tongue for all,
the voice of the group
and I am empowered to say
what they would say,
and what I want, they would want.

I have been chosen
to look you in the eye
and make clear to you at last
that unless you move toward our position
we're not moving toward yours.
Around this table, the water jug,
the styrofoam cups, the loosened ties,
the pads of paper are all
waiting for you.

Yes, you're getting paid
and we are not, are in fact
cold and wrestling with sickness
in the dark of the picket line—but let it rain:
the elements will keep us
on track: start with the language
in article 3.04
and then move forward until we stop—
and at that point let us dance
—sometimes you leading, sometimes me,
offering, rejecting,
breaking to rewrite and whisper.
Come now, my colleagues are cold,
and I hear them shuffling and stamping
in the street.

RHETORIC

Ours is not the only strike
in the news: one man
has been dragged by a truck;
outside movie theatres
trade unionists have lined up.
These strikes
bring out the heavyweights.

We talk of escalation,
and others from the province
bring greetings
of support—as if we are sick,
wrapped up, in hospital,
recovering from a fall.

At the back of the hall
someone will cry out
for secret ballot
but there is no time now.
The electric will
runs through us again:
we have the right
to withdraw
our labour.

We have the right . . .
We have the right . . .

These words ring in me,
give and take
what I myself might think,
and which later I must find
in the dark before sleep
when the thug of my tongue
is calmed, held down,
healed,
lightened.

THREE WISHES

That I may grow
another room (hidden from all)
into which I step and leave behind
where the neighbourhood
skateboards prowl
and the citizens
writhing sea to sea
write their MPs.

For my neighbour:
that he might hold his rearview
mirror less lovingly
as he wipes his car today;
that he direct himself away
from mechanization and
spin inward, elsewhere
and come to greet me then;
that we could speak, and I perhaps
would know him better.

I travel to work
and I see from the train
a man working construction below.
I cannot see his face,
he is only inches tall,
his arms held high in the air hour after hour
receiving loads of steel
from the cranes above.
I wish him to be
an archangel of happiness toward which
the burden of our hearts may start to flow.

POEM FACING EVENING

1.

One morning you get up
let the cat in—
and a story, tune,
movement exactly let loose
from what waits to come
presents its face:

> I could be gunning the outside lane
> making my turn to go home
>
> I could be standing at the window
> an apple in my hand
>
> or at night when the sky is black
> and a void worth falling into
>
> my children fall asleep
> ahead of schedule, just for me
>
> a book leaps down
> I had better pay attention there as well
>
> a hand is turning over
> my heart, looking under a stone
>
> the eye takes in its city
> and isn't much of a judge
>
> I could be sliding down a hill
> and fail to negotiate the slope
>
> be standing where the ocean
> rolls in its great question.

You head out the door
charged by just plain air,
you punch
and suck it up—and later
blood and eyes and lips
move downtown-fast all day.

Or you could bend
over a spoon—
and the soup gets cold:

> If I had a hat, I could arrest
> myself each morning
>
> when I was a child I felt
> new feeling every day
>
> open my umbrella in the first
> fall rain and there it is again
>
> I could be reading the Saturday
> paper and hear someone cry
>
> my children the perfect disguise
> and my wife a great coat
>
> anywhere isn't exactly a place
> but the heart knows nothing of that
>
> in the evening when you have perhaps

no will to resist
and you jackknife onto
the couch: a moment, maybe
two when you breathe,
relax—before sleep
makes you grump upstairs
your block quietening down—

you drift
in the fragments, some of which
came that close to you
falling out of nowhere
just to warm your blood.

2.

The country is filling up
with poets like him. People emigrate
and become poets the moment they arrive.

What makes a country think
it has this much to say?
A wind circles the planet
every hundred years.
It's back now: in Canada
one in four is touched.
Poets who don't even want to
are scribbling on the buses
trying to keep the lines in their heads
until coffee and then
the boss speaks.
Poets who teach:
they get chalk in their poems
and questions in their theories.
They arrive back at their desks and
the real work walks out the door—
Look, if you're not interested just now . . . .
Poets who climb mountains and
cling to the edge until the language
is purified again.
Poets who wear Birkenstocks.

                Women, men
poets with personalities
thrown up on billboards.
Poets without a word-hoard.
Poets for peace, for research,
for the love of language.
Some have used up all their
capital
s, others have hidden agendas
for their neighbourhoods
and are satisfied
just to have a group of friends
think they are in touch with
a certain influence beyond carport
barbecues.

Poets who think coffee
helps and a routine but not too much alcohol.
Poets who really believe in the paper
and not in the poem,
the ones who need to see ink,
the ones who have given up.
The poets who haven't yet
been born and will come to air
with the words around them
surfacing in the world of metaphor
which is the real one (poets say).

   The dead ones
who said it for their time
and hooked us into thinking
they said it forever, it was that good
and no one ever once called it
stuff. The old poems we return to
when we need to return.
Poets who secretly wish

they were novelists,
had word-processors and characters
lined along the hall to the bathroom.
Poets who sicken and get worse
because the word is like that.
Poets who prevail
when their brothers make a killing
in real estate,
when their children get visual
and drop out of books altogether
—they can lose their faith
just by looking out the window,
seeing trees and another person
not like them.

The daily poem keeps waiting.
The poets are gunning for it
determined to flush it out
and what they thought was a gazelle
is a charging thing with hides
that can't be penetrated.
On headlands overlooking the sea
poets are waiting
for wind; in waterbeds
they embrace the coming of the poem,
its hot breath the meaning
one in four roll out toward
presses, publishers.

These crazy ones,
the ones with Rilke's eyes now,
the brooders
but not the broken-
down half angry ones—not the
dying-down old ones who have gambled
their blood on words and say such things
they can't help themselves anymore.
In rest homes somewhere a nurse
isn't listening,
their kids gone away into life
and the language like a brook at spring
in their minds, but their tongues
thick as roots and their hands arthritic,
the technology not ready
to cut straight into the brainflow.

Poets who have more than one theme!
Poets out in the air, on a sunny day,
on horses, riding through the fields.
Poets in old cars
on the freeway.

A poet stuck
     waiting for the perfect word
     in which the world can be breathed
     out, cleansing the neighbourhood

     and maybe he is right about that.

Poets who are finally afraid
of poetry, and yet
poets who give what flows and try not to be
corrupt. Poets who outnumber the odds
against them. One on your street,
three or four in your supermarket
checking the meat and potatoes,
the South American bananas.
In your liquor store
avoiding wines from
politically incorrect places.
At your gas station, expect them
to come driving in. Sometimes

eating at the table next to you,
alive in your shadow
catching what you thought
had gone (by),
the knock and the elbows
in the room around you

building
out of the air you breathe.

3.

So the poem went banging
on the doors of the city and was not heard.
The poem flew up the hill to Academics
and was fed to fire,
could not find its place
it seems   it seems not   it seems
and it reached out to a book
lay down on the page,
the smell of new and glue overcoming
the nose pressed in close to the V
—let's sup
said the poem, on the alphabet, be drunk!

This social realist poem had to have friends.
In the book it went unnoticed.
In the biggest book by all the poets
it was not worth mentioning
said the Critic—and the poem left off
in a huff. You can see for yourself
that white page at the end,
a shadow of type remains.
Ink spilled and left its half behind
when the poem lifted off in its desire
to be the greatest.

If you see that mutilated poem
some night, it will be pale
and visible, caught
crossing your lawn. Report what you can,
don't open the door   boot
the reject and go back to your
dinner and wit—but
speak a little louder or stand
near to the window. Your good words
may yet fall into the night

solace the thing where it
crouches under the ledge
caught up in
such inadequacies,
such plans for the moon.
The poem gives up its breath,
exhales no ambiguities, is dead at last.
And in the library inside the house, not far
from the room with the beautiful tongues
a page is read and turned
as if nothing were there.
Dead again
and every day still dying.

APHASIA

AFTERNOON AND EVENING

The woman who has been married three times
dreams she has no name; the man who lives for Sunday
dreams he is three men. The child might dream
one colour
that isn't in the rainbow.
I wake up worried I have slipped
a deadline;
I leap to the window, looking for time,
and see crows
already gathered in the far woods
raking their hearts together into a pile.

*

She's taking seventeen pills a day. At least one of them
is making her voice waver as if she's deaf
so when I listen on the phone and she talks to me
half a continent away, it's underwater talk.
My youngest on the line.
As for me I'm focusing on the hallway,
the door at the end,
the smell of the pay-phone in my hand,
all the troubles poured into its mouth. Later
propped on the bed, I might shout what rushes us:
the doors blown open,
cats from childhood hunched up hissing, wind
where the fire used to be.

APHASIA

It is the suddenness of crossing
over
that cannot be comprehended.
One moment she is among us
reaching for her purse . . . .

The nurses clean and cuddle,
talk numbers—
b.p. one-ten-over-sixty—
and these we babble to friends
and those givers of ill advice,
hours when the smells are
not our own, even children
quietening down
in the sudden blow of dumbness
where she lives.

After a journey of many simplicities
we spy her still
alone, at a great distance, immobile
behind that other number
none can guess. We practice
contact
but she cannot

at first   we smash up
inside   all night
after the hours of visitation have safely
passed and the dark leads us
away. Alone on the ward
she hunts for *bed*
car teeth   comb.

FLYING BACK FROM SOLEMN DUTIES

Waves of geese breaking
and re-forming
in the September air
full of their south-calling—
and beneath them
the pull of the intravenous
and the beds stained, the trays dropped.

The women in white warned
—Look at her chest
which eventually did not rise
to take the air
held by modern windows
as if deciding at last
about the worthiness of a moment.

Thursday morning
we crowd together in our good
dark clothes,
sit and admire
the church window
shining, clouds in the west piling,
and every pew filled
—and later, the faces
blown about by winds

much like the jet
is knocked about
on this last trip, the ladies of the aisle
gracious and weary
bending down to ask of comfort,
aware we have come through miles
to be up in the rocking air

and the man beside me starts
to talk and knows immediately
that I am not willing
and he turns back to
folding a newspaper, eating a bag of nuts
and thus together
we make a space around us
as we descend.

TOP DRAWER

When your brother decides to marry
a Catholic, you don't care,
but your parents are mortified
—and you realize being twelve
has some responsibility,
and you try explaining to your mother
what it means to have another church
over your head with the same God
looking down—right? But she's
ironing shirt after shirt from
the damp clothes pile, and she says
it isn't her she's worried about, it's
him again, my father, who's
unable to accept, and my mother says
he's not talking.

Ten years later, then
twenty years later, grandchildren
are poking up and no one talks
about that time, not even me—
why should I bother to mention it now?
We've just gone through the albums again,
and I've seen myself standing
in that row of men and women,
my father in the front pew with flowers
in his lapel, and his wife beside him
smiling in turquoise—and both
are faking something.

So it's twenty years, and now
spread across the table in the kitchen
is what's left. We've got no choice
but to sort out the contents
of her dresser drawer, what falls
through the years
into such places: letters, junk jewels, one glove.
Take it away, someone says, but
the grandchildren are eager to see
what it must have been like to wear
such things, and they fondle them
and try them on, and their parents say
Yes, you should have that,
she would have wanted you to have that.

Those kids, already looking
far ahead, prancing and full of plans.
Who they marry perhaps will matter.
My brothers and I chat
and divide the keepsakes.
This may be one of the very last things
ever said for a while, here
where the silence of our father descends
and the mother's tongue
stirs and stirs—but can't break through.

SINS OF OMISSION

One morning
when your family is out
and you are alone with yourself,
your mother walks into your room
and you see her old feet
curling with arthritic flame.
Afterward it is clear she wanted
speech from you to take up
where the death of her husband
had stopped her path.
But just then
you could say nothing.

We meet in our lives
friend, child, worker,
love—and next?
Death will be
a true-life adventure, so gripping
we won't get away.
We are afraid. Imagine
the awaiting roll call of sins,
a friend who fell from you
as if you were driving fast
and her billboard were moving away.

DAVID DALE

Forced to abandon him
by a grade one teacher who could not accept
two boys with the same name, I accepted
my second. I think of David
as a skin dropped, a ball
lost in the summer grass.

My parents often spoke of him
or mouthed my new name
as if I were a guest
and they were waiting politely
for his return

—because what faults I had
could never spring from him.
Well, did he grow up
through change, embarrassment,
and try to speak the lines
reserved after all for him? He never did.

When I meet him now
at dawn or just before sleep, he stands
speechless although I know he wants from me
more than words.

Lately, when I cut myself
on paper, and the sharp red line wells over
and falls, his young mouth
is pressed against my hand.

SIBLING RIVALRY

My youngest ends up crying.
I wade into the pinching,
and expect to live, but where's the peace
I thought the centre of all
good families? I mimicked my brother
until we were both
sent away from the table.
Everything was fine
until you came along.

And later the baby
of the family is the very last
to fall: the youngest
buries mother, father,
brothers all knocked down.

—Will I curl under institutional
blankets, and travel
down into the first world of mother's skin,
a brother's unkind shove?

Some days they hold me to this bed
or pull me up so very far
I think someone is waiting.

DEBBIE'S PIANO

Certainly things will pass
out of your life and you won't miss
some heartache you catch your
breath against
at first and then   how soon
even the memory can't spring out of you
in palpitations.
But some stay to haunt: how foolish
to let *that* go—to
a stranger's hand,
dank basement, attic of dust
broken up for fire what once
held a child—but
—older—wanting nothing
material—then Debbie's piano
passed out of the home
and no one remembers how,
now they no longer have
the house to hold it, nor
the girl who came up from the beach
towel-slow and sat
to play
and turned to look at you
with her grin.

VIOLENCE

Always someone's stone
falls nearby. The fly I couldn't chase
out of the house still crashes
between blind and pane.
I resign myself
to folding news across my lap,
to legs up, tinged blue,
and the window's perfect frame.

We are forever carving on the skins
of our children
the way we live. Imagine
back in the country, pleased
at first to pet the goat
which later is hauled away
where children aren't to know
(except perhaps in dreams)
the whack and spilling at the seams.

After the heavy rain here
the rocks in the creek
grind against the slopes
earth dares to bring down.

THE MOTHER PRONE ✦

Now I'm off my feet
I can't tell who's
opening and closing
the fridge.
I could sleep today
as I have often come to sleep
hands folded over
these flattened breasts
which have done with sons
—or Frank, preoccupied I guess
now the boys are gone, or only home
with guests.
You would have thought
comfort in each other
had more to give than food,
an Eaton's chesterfield,
abstract art above my head.
Afternoon light

makes a poor place to come to.
Louise across the street
has taken pills; Diane has dyed her hair.
A new car in the driveway
helps, as does volunteer work.
Someone should come to my door now.
I should just
get up, not nurse
this sinking or I'll fall
farther through this wealth
of foam and carpet and hard-
wood floors, and into the ground.
What could balance
the cost of repairs
my family would have to make then?
As it is, we're painting
this year, Frank says
—no holiday in him.

ADVISING ++

Louise came by today and left me
black again: I tried to say
remember trees still grow
on the farm where you once lived
—they couldn't seem to move
until the night wind came.
You worried as a child
that green would blow away
and every fall it did.
That's how it is sometimes.
You close the door, and there's a man
inside, taking
all the window or all the bed.
But here it's morning, look,
the coffee's good: make plans
to read a book.
Take in a show
and leave the work for him.

Or not—I think
what else I could have said.
Regret's no way to make your face.
Give him the shove tonight
and keep the key.
Don't stick it out.
You'll end up dry and hard.
You know the women on this block
think you've got luck;
they're looking at your hollyhocks
and marvelling again.
You've got good earth.
New weather's always moving in.
—Instead I saw your hands
and what each said, what makes them shake
and why they're always
plunging in the ground out there
each spring.

READING LATE ✦✦✦

Frank's standing in my light
—his rumpled hair—and saying
please come to bed.
I take the book into the kitchen,
lay it on the table—and it feels
the family I have fed.
I want the book to understand
that I will know its drama
in the quiet of the nothing times.
Perhaps one day the book will tell
the story of a mother's voice
that went away
and when a boy sits down in years to come
touches wood such as this
light such as this
the smell of breakfast
filling his head . . . .
Pacing room to room

makes sure the goblins
don't get in.
One moment more to latch the screen
while streetlights turn the lawn to blue.
From thrillers to biography
I sometimes think—Her At The Door—
come in, come in.
Your company is good, my husband's
gone to bed again—remember how
the boys sat up and cried aloud—if so
you go and water them.
I can't hear just now, am
far down the hall, free at the table
where pages turn
half dark by night
half lit by what I've got within
—the villain of the piece
no doubt tomorrow.

REMEMBERING FRANK ✦✦✦✦

Inside of me the word was
Yes, this man will soothe away
those other chumps who climbed too fast.
That day, his hat against the sun,
the picnic full of heat
and later in the night a dance
—three girls for every man around
and half of them straight pokers, oh sweet
at first the moonlight on their skin
till later when they'd rise and hate
the place they'd been, loose-limbed
in you: no easy time for girls back then.
But Frank—he didn't bother with
the grope: he was tucked tight.
I thought his mother must have said
beware of certain things—the heat,
the night, his car along the river road,
a chance for quickie sin.

And now the story goes (we laugh)
he'd crossed the floor for someone else
when I stood up and
startled up his life.
He never dreamed three boys
were walking with him then—I saw
them catching at his shirt and as we danced
not smooth but bumping on the floor
among their many hands
I heard them mew.
                                    Later
in a country unprotected—
what loss, what gain
this hanging onto men
—who come and go from me
and leave the dishes still undone
not knowing I too
am travelling where I am.

POSTSCRIPT: SARAH ✦✦✦✦✦

On the way to Zellers to buy
sale things—or even
as I walk by certain cluttered yards
I glimpse just who she might have been,
my girl the light strikes down upon
—and mush comes loose inside.
But three were all
that came to me—who knows
what worlds we never see.
I never speak this way to anyone.
Who wouldn't sneer
among these aisles of cotton tops
to see my mother's heart pulled out.
A mother tugs along her cart;
ice cream drips from baby's chin.
There's love in that.
—And I've had Maxwell, Bill,
and silly grinning Jim.

Or had them, and they had me.
We settled into war and love.
That's done: no more secrets out of them.
My childless friends hold photographs
propped here and there
throughout the house, and say:
how nice, how sad, how sweet
the luck they've given me.
And yes I understand the gifts
each can bring—and happy to be through
with socks inside the dryer,
that sweet old static cling.
Yet she is somewhere—on nights
when they return I open wide the drapes,
let moon pour down across
their twisting sleeping shapes
each like their dad, each certain
tough heat will help them win.

THE WEIGHT OF MY RAGGEDY SKIN

HEART TAKES

*

He wakes up to a watch
ticking, the sun's
streaming in: June and already
a man whistling outside,
the day almost begun without him
until he sees his arm
hanging just there, his hand and hair
and where the pulse is leading
downstairs to the cool ground.
Saturday morning and the kitchen's bare.

*

It's noisy here at the centre
with valves flying open and shut.
We're at the border no one's crossed
yet—but a crew is ready.
"Excuse me, how does it feel,
the first to be going up the Aorta?"
"It's the Nile all over again, up there
a weather we can't predict
—or worse—a whole bothersome continent
of light."

*

I have to call across
the country again.
I have to find out the news
about someone's heart, in the
hospital. First I untangle
the phone, dangling it
so it twirls and stops.
I check the number one last time

and wait.

*

Two kinds of hearts in the world,
those that work and those other
stopped ones. Can't make *them* sigh
or laugh, can't make light
of undelivered letters to the dead.
They come back and you open them
and live. Or leave them
in the bottom drawer,
find them later
imploding with regret.

*

You on the other side of the screen
I can't believe what you say.
You'd sell the light
I'm following
straight through the hole
into the tangle of wires, nests,
what your brain is
when it shifts
and sighs all night
through heart's prime time.

*

How did I get out here
throbbing away on this sleeve?
Now every eye
smiles so smugly down at me.
When do I get back
to pipes and tubes, the dark
I press and pump.
How long to master
my gait, and that bastard
adrenalin coming when I'm half asleep.

*

"Father Away On Business Trip,
Mother Dies From 'Flu,
Six-Month-Old Alone For Two Days."
Such stories!—can't be true
can they? In the basement of the newsroom
some blackheart—
A neighbour would have heard
the woman's cries. She did cry
didn't she? *The mailman* . . .
but already he is turning away.

*

The gargoyles in this city
hang off the bridges,
can't be seen unless you're
driving fast, under the influence:
booze, drugs, a heart in the trunk,
bent for the airport.
Here's Security. Smile,
stay blank, not beating
or the faces deep
in your pockets beep and come alive.

*

Those who find no consolation
in the world must eat
their own hearts.
Those who have brought forward
no stone from their father's house
will need to borrow
only in flesh, but in time
such a dwelling
is always a poor one
—and all there ever is.

*

Look to the mouth—you'll find
the crooked pout that says
no satisfaction and can't deny
how the world has failed.
Down at the corners, everyone
sags, drool lines deepening
until the sour side of the day
makes a permanent mark
on that outside heart
where we kiss.

*

The association of genitals and
hands is a daily one.
We know these things develop
and are comfortable.
But where's the place you can touch
so simply
and not feel
some lesion in the flesh
making its way home?
How do you wipe that clean?

*

Attic work: high clutter
of dolls, frames
without faces.
Not just the refused
parts of ourselves, unconnected
jumble we hooked to our hearts
and pumped out
—but this chair,
each time we enter, remembering
who I was.

*

Cantilever his heart
some old carpenter god.
Take a ladder out on a limb
if you need to, make a strong place
where you can launch it
into a river, a big Asian river.
Watch it wobble and flop,
a boomerang
an old pet
fresh from rolling in the muck.

*

I'm under the influence of myself again.
I used to squat down
at the edge of some great fire
—the hero leaping up
bangles on his arm—
but the left-handed chamber
didn't surrender, and out of it runs
who I thought I gave away: ordinarily
no matter where you go
there you are.

*

Good thing I'm not God.
I'd strike you down,
Martin Luther, Mr. Calvin: come
back and take the devil out of me,
you put him there.
I'm letting him out little by little
at my children,
my heart against the wall,
some good woman at the door
wanting money for the poor and the sick.

*

Whose heart isn't a terror
jumping up, dear,
when you finger a label
in the most chic of shops,
a best dress lining you up.
Then as you go by the benches,
the men
turn their beams on you
and hearts leap
into the ashtray's white sand.

*

The mist along the creek falls
on every bud.
Foolishness took me to the banks
and stood me up to wait.
That spring rushed so hard
rocks rumbled under the waves.
It's scarcely worth a mention now
but the heart's jump turned me around,
on my face the damp measure of things
always out to continue.

*

The neighbour of the poet
hears tac in the night,
the talking hammer
of his machine, and she turns
away from that
shared wall. Morning he might
shout his heart
up the stairs,
wife, kids. All other times
on his own.

JOURNEY

Mouth is the closest you will get
to myself:
wet, dark, red
with a thing that lives.

I could disappear
into my mouth
—goodbye, it's worth it, here I come.
I live here now,

feel all around
impatience,
the flapping quickness
and the opening and closing to the light.

Further back
peril, a descent
and the hollow sounding
of a drum.

The running sound, too,
of many tributaries
linking, far off
so at night, drowned

in dreams, I slide out
and thus escape
and make my way back
to the closed eye,

entrance way to the caverns.
Here dream convolutions
too difficult to explain
are spotted and sent

down where leverage
to the tongue is strongest
—but as yet unable to speak
for the weight of my raggedy skin.

HOROSCOPE

"You have to struggle with the world,
the flesh and the devil"—it said
in that little book
size of a prayer manual
less than a dollar
at any check-out.
Toss it in the bag.
Then unpack frozen veggies and
juice, and right there on the kitchen floor
grapple with
that black hole—
always keeps you guessing—
when will it pull you in?
My family would think immediately
of the holidays:
the sea, the kids, the sand
kept getting on me.

As for the flesh—
I should be able to handle who I am.
Isn't that the basic line we've all been given?
To live our lives—and know our lives—
and sit in the chairs we've brought,
and read the little words
that throw up their hands to say
You are possessed by the needs of others
this week, and you will abuse them:
as you stagger toward loved ones,
find new opportunities.
Do not fail.

HERE ON THE COAST

. . . it is the dead
who speak to us
from the water
and from the trees.

Dark inlet,
you invite me under,
you keep saying
another waits.

Since we know
water alone
cannot speak so clearly
whose dead

does the sojourner
hear? His own,
made precious by absence?
The ones who call to him
always when he comes near water?

Or some other
who mistakes his melancholic
way for a heart.

Then the trees call:
from their bases,
fluted mouths to the ground,
they are taking up
into the sky

their entangling love
of the air.

STORIES OF LOATHING

The man re-rooted in the flesh of his love
appears now on her stairs
—but the light slants down from laughs
and stains his face deep red.
Rustle of skin above
clears his thinking out,
and he hears the deep low
of the loathing.
Now you're the man with the smile
who knows his neighbour
as a further self
awash with fantasy.
The neighbourhood at dusk
switches on
the interior floods.
You're the man clutches himself
through the night,
the woman who pats and
winks, genuflects before the altar
of every other woman,
cuts to the fridge:
low blood sugar
meets low self-esteem,
and your kids
bear you
through the queenly gloom.

                        Sleep
paints out the worst of it,
or alcohol, at first a trumpet
then a drone,
deepens out
and says you're home.

THE MAN WITH THE LAWN MOWER

1.

The man with the lawn mower
cannot hear if a woodpecker
calls him from the ravine; a slow
tapping telegram says stop.
In his cocoon of sound
he vibrates deeper into the green

and cannot hear his neighbours
deride his flowerbeds:
the occasional weed has taken hold.
The man does not care.
"Why should I? Why should I?"

In the morning before the street
bristles, he climbs
into his tallest tree, pulls himself
high as nerves will go,
higher than branches might allow
if they were flesh.

He hears a neighbour
slam out; a mother breaks down a child
with the affection of a hunter
opening his gun. A dog howls
what the child can't say.

On his way down
the pores on the white trunk
close up.

2.

He's yelling—and she's
just standing on the stairs.
The kids need food/sleep/love
clothes and cleanliness.
Sometimes they're a team
and the job gets done; in the hour
at the end, they sit
speechless, fighting what sleeps.
Or (him) complaining:
his lack of nerve, his wanting more,
how he would grow old and be
dead—and she looks up from knitting,
saying this but not to him,
"I guess that's coming."

Her needles weave around,
make things worth leaving:
the toys they've
put away, clothes they can't
give up. Also
who isn't listening
when each other's version of the day
runs shapeless through the room,
     phantasm with his mouth
     her endurance
     children's quick getaway.

THE SHADOW . . .

is situated partly in the personal
unconscious, the regions of memories and repressions, and
is connected with the less attractive parts of our life history.
—Bernard Lievegoed, *Phases*

Glen said to his friends
I am going down into the basement
to meet my shadow
—and he did.
When he came up
his smile was leering
and he immediately entered a manic phase.
His friends at first
would not believe
his transformation, and then
they drove him from the house.
It is not possible to live with madness
too long.

Glen released himself
to his parents,
who were fundamentally opposed
to such liberation; they blamed
his friends, who in turn laughed
at the blindness in the old folks
when in front of them
danced not the devil they imagined but the child
they'd forced. Glen's sister
cried because her brother had left her
behind and his father thundered in the night
and his mother remained committed
to the ways of her mother.

Look in the mirror some night
—Glen says—and glimpse behind you
all the desires you've left undone,
and with your will, make a shape.
No need for gruesome werewolf faces
—Glen says, now he's under medication—
your own face
reflects fire enough.
When later captured and returned
is always twisted off the mark,
having given up the bond
that wants to work
                 with others
and succeed.

STORIES FROM THE LIFE OF FLESH

1.

Judy wanted most of all
—to get out of school
and getting pregnant
flung her out the doors forever.
Her teacher, last to know,
stands before the class,
back to the board;
an escarpment rises gently
whenever he steps out
as if just the moment before
he had wished for relief.

One hot day in June
when the work was at an end
and he had spoken of (nothing but)
history and war and the
essay—she tilted sideways
and fainted, melting out of her desk
to the floor.
All grade eleven
tittered:
knocked up, their phrase
the violent prologue to birth.

Leave a place you're born to
and then return—
a lot comes undone. That child
tugs them off the fields
and into the stores,
finds a name for himself
in the town, moves on. In history
such a moment is rarely recorded:
what kind of treaty is made
with your son
when he's as hard
as your man, that other soul
always there for you
now, but at first
the welcome assailant.

2.

The itinerant worker's son
tells how his father
came upon a woman one day,
and from the look between them
there was also a child, now this man
simplifying his life and his
father's life.

The worker with his hat twisted
into his pocket, jumps
from the rolling train,
a sudden flash of white,
one roll of clothes, dust in his teeth.

Watch low mountains
spread away from that man.
They whisper to him
step into the long picture
where the woman turns to trace
beside her pillow
the heat of the summer

that even now their son can feel
along the golden hairs of his arm,
in the curve of his spine on the chair.
Although he cannot recall
leaning out of the future,
a life of flesh before him.

3.

He had no sense
that the black man and the
tool-push hated each other
enough to use their break
fighting by the small back door,
audience leaning
on corrugated tin.

The fight itself
no better than any male slammer
—one man cocky
then hitting another's head
on the frozen ground.

Stepping from light
back to work,
the bright machines
firing, buzzing,
foreman appears suddenly
to warn about productivity
and fitting screws in the maw
where nozzles of paint
turn carcasses of tin
man-made red.

Then your own hands
where you slipped against the wrench
and dug knuckles, and wringing them
still, everyone gathers now
to piss and wash up,
intent on grease.

DESTROYER OF ATMOSPHERES

. . . mighty and weighty,
one of the ancients
riding blue off the horizon.
Out of the Bible's back pages,
out of the parts left over
once the animals awoke from sleep
to discover thump in their chests,
the light touch of the god constantly
reminding them to whom
they owed their allegiance.
How complex they became
and we came
even more divinely convoluted:
the destroyer of atmospheres
has begat you, and all around
but rapidly disappearing
the shimmer of the burst that fell
upon the world
and sent women off to the wells.

Night vision was given
to a special few: owl and wolf,
hunters at the edge of the burgeoning.
When we huddle together,
arguing still how to
block off the cave, we can hear
night workers pull at the edges
of the scheme. This is the way
we have come to see things,
we who see
into the dark but cannot find
the spark that sets the conflagration
going. I nudge my neighbour,
anticipate my partner.
I listen for the wind that might mean
we are about to be recalled,
remodelled again to fit
what's mighty, weighty
too.

WINTER RESIDENCE

The bright day
leaps out of autumn,
out of the warping we do
when the day fills with rain;
and we always look inward, never guessing right.

But this day the clouds are high
and summer-white, spectators watching earth,
and earthlings out to enjoy.

The light that breaks with fall
slants against our eye
eager to penetrate flesh,
proclaiming no other way except our own.
We are the winter residence of light.

Elementals have joined today
to offer
a grand turning; not the moment dull and
everlasting (as cold can be, as heat
pronounces on and on until we're weak)—

but the signal earth,
now cool, now fresh,
and in the comfort of the long shadows, the pause
upholding the crimson leaf.

THE DEAD ARE WITH US

How many generations
look through the gauzy frame
that separates them from colour
and from us?

If your father
is watching you reach for the glass
in the same way he once did
so what
and what can he do?

Send electronically
some premonition
or shiver that breaks the way time
always seems to pass
at a rate so slowly
it cannot be seen?

Is he turning out
wildly less
than his plans—if that moment
is realized not from within

but from without,
the unseen visitor
touching
and making him see
around the brain's fiery tree

some dark
never guessed before—
invisible? Down a path
past all familiar stations
where old volition ends.

ACCIDENT

Remember that girl
decapitated by a ladder diving
off a carpenter's truck
as she drove home.
To study. Flop down on the sofa
before hitting the books, smacking
Jane Eyre a good one, unwilling to believe
so much misfortune and trembling
at the edge outside
in the garden. And as the ambulance
gathers its loved ones together
at the end of the bridge
where we slow for the reassuring
glance at death

                another woman
waits for the heavy man
to come down, and as she lifts
to take his weight
and love cries out
tingling in the air,
she is bothered by insistence
coming closer, nearby. When he has gone
tumbling out of bed again
after the long pause and the lifting away
she feels the sun shining
in another room, and from that world
—it dawns on her—comes a visitor
journeying her way.

Printed on paper
containing over 50%
recycled paper including
5% post-consumer fibre.

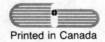

Printed in Canada